500+ Fun & Fascinating
Hockey Facts for Kids

Discover Mind-Blowing, Educational, and Surprising Ice Hockey Facts for Young Champions!

Fenix Publishing

"To the future hockey stars, may this book ignite your passion for the game and fuel your curiosity. Here's to endless hours of learning, laughter, and love for the sport."

Alex Harper

Want **FREE BOOKS** for the rest of your LIFE?

Join our VIP club now by scanning the QR code to get **FREE** access to all our future books.

We ONLY send you an email when we launch a NEW BOOK. NO SPAM. Never. Ever!

Just an email with **YOUR 100% OFF COUPON CODE**.

CONTENTS

Part IV

Stars on Ice: Tales of Hockey Heroes, Prodigies, and Legends......57

Part V

Hockey Chronicles: Legends, Rivalries, and Frozen Feats............80

Your Opinion Matters to Us!

We put our heart and soul into writing this book and made sure that every piece of information contained within it is 100% accurate. We thoroughly research, reference, and review all content before making any definitive statements. Although we have included facts that we believe are most helpful and interesting for hockey lovers, we do want to hear your thoughts, opinions, critical analysis, and support after you've read the book. This will not only boost our confidence but also restore the energy that we put into our hard work.

We are happy and excited to present **500+ Fun & Fascinating Hockey Facts for Kids** to you, and we truly hope that this book increases your knowledge about the game. It is 100% safe to read and is recommended for hockey-loving kids.

At our small publishing company, we have a deep love for hockey, and we highly appreciate the feedback we receive from our readers. The opinions and comments of hockey enthusiasts like you are utterly important to us, as they help us improve our content and ensure that we always meet your expectations. We truly value your engagement, and we look forward to hearing from you.

Introduction

Rise and shine, little champs, and welcome to the world of hockey, where the ice is cold but the excitement is red-hot! We will dive into the core of the game in this fun-filled journey, covering everything from its early history to the amazing feats of modern-day champions. Get ready for a slap shot of information sprinkled with a dash of entertainment as we unearth more than 500 fantastic hockey facts that will make young champions cheer for more!

Do not think that hockey is just a game; it is a passion and emotion passed down through generations. The history of hockey is as rich as the taste of victory, from the icy ponds of the past to the high-energy feels of modern times. As Wayne Gretzky, the legendary "Great One," once said, "Hockey is a unique sport in the sense that you need every guy helping each other and pulling in the same direction to be successful."

Buckle up, little fellows, as we skate through time to uncover the origins of this fantastic sport. To quote Jim McKenny, the legendary Canadian ice hockey player, "Half the game is mental; the other half is being mental."

You have to be present on the field, not just physically but mentally, too. It means you must have the right and precise mindset for every move you make in the game. Be aware of the possible steps of your opponent and plan a strategy accordingly. My little pals, there is a lot to learn about hockey, and you have picked just the right guide for it.

Can you believe there was a time when frozen ponds with sticks carved from branches were the hockey game venue instead of sleek arenas? Surprised, right? The early days of hockey were an indication of the resilience and creativity of players. You will be blown away by how this humble game, born on icy surfaces, grew into the powerhouse of athleticism we know today.

Did you know that the history of hockey contains more than just victories and goals? Details of innovation, determination, and, of course, a good deal of amusing moments are a big part of it as well. Imagine this: players would use sticks made from tree branches and carved wooden blocks, serving as pucks. It feels like the original hockey players were crafting their magic wands to cast spells on the ice.

But that's just a start, my little fellows. In this book you will explore the tales surrounding the origins of indoor hockey, the evolution of goalie gear, and the international popularity of the sport. We will learn about the history of the National Hockey League (NHL), the pinnacle of professional hockey, and stories of the Stanley Cup—the recognizable trophy that has been the subject of victories and heartbreaks for more than a century.

The science behind skating is amazing and also the comebacks will make you to hold your breath. You will find yourself at the edge of your seat and biting your nails with excitement. There are also inspirational tales of strong women who have made names for themselves in the hockey community. We will peek into the minds of legendary coaches, learn intriguing facts about hockey equipment, and see how generosity and kindness play a significant role in this exciting sport.

So let's not wait anymore, grab your favorite hockey jersey, put on your game, and get ready for a roller coaster ride of facts and fun. This book is more than simply a hockey-playing guide; it is your behind-the-scenes pass to the world of hockey, where every page is a new goal waiting to be scored. And yes, do not forget to put on your skates, lace them up, and join the puck party. Let's hit the ice, young champs!

Part I

Hockey Horizons: From Frozen Past to Golden Present

You know, every big story always has a beginning. Every big sport, every great man, every tasty food, and every beautiful place was once hidden, undiscovered, unknown, and undeveloped. Similarly, hockey, no matter how famous or fascinating a game it may be, was once unknown to the world. To know about its origins, I will take you 4,000 years back in time. So prepare your backpacks, fill up the water bottles, and put on those sunglasses as we get on board this journey.

The late Duke of Clarence playing Hockey at Cambridge.

Hockey and Its History

Long, long ago, on planet Earth, way before the advent of smartphones, cool toys, and video games, the people of Ethiopia played hockey around 1,000 BC, the Egyptians 4,000 years ago, and the Iranians played the super early version of hockey around 2,000 BC. Can you imagine? They were having icy adventures over 4,000 years ago (History of Hockey | FIH, n.d.)! Now, let's hear some fun facts about the history of hockey.

1. The Greeks, ancient Romans, and Aztecs had their own version of the game before Christopher Columbus discovered America.

2. The modern version of hockey first popped up in England in the 18th century.

3. Hockey played a significant role in the growth and development of public schools such as Eton.

4. Surprisingly, in 1876, a bunch of hockey-loving friends in the U.K. formed the first-ever association in hockey and created some ground rules (Gillis, 1996).

5. Although this association remained in power for six years, only in 1866 did it make a big comeback, with nine clubs joining the fun. So, kids, that is how the fantastic journey of hockey officially started.

6. The word "hockey" was once called "hoquet" in French, which translates to "shepherd's crook."

7. Originally, pucks were made of wood blocks, and balls were also used as temporary pucks.

8. In Montreal in 1875, the first indoor hockey game was like unwrapping a treasure chest.

9. Goalies relied on skill and courage in the past; they were brave knights without the fancy uniforms of today.

10. Early goalies guarded the net with minimal gear, much like real-life magicians.

11. The Stanley Cup is as old as your great-great-grandparents, making it the ultimate hockey prize. It was established in 1893 (Diamond et al., 2003).

12. The earliest leg pads used by goaltenders in hockey were inspired by cricket pads.

13. They were made from leather and filled with deer hair and sometimes kapok, which is used in life jackets on ships (Ice Hockey Goaltending Equipment, 2023).

14. In 1917, the National Hockey League (NHL) made its debut and turned hockey into a major league of its own.

15. Hockey even featured on the Olympic stage in 1920.

The Wildest Comebacks

We all love comebacks as they keep us on the edge of our seats, increase our heartbeat, captivate our minds, and make the events unforgettable. Similarly, hockey does contain a box full of amazing comebacks that will excite you every time you watch or read about them.

16. One of the finest comebacks happened in 2009 when the Bruins, who were running behind 3 goals, made a remarkable comeback against the Canadians.

17. This comeback was no less than a Hollywood climax when the Kings were behind 5-0 going into the "Miracle on Manchester" in 1982, but they rallied to win 6-5.

18. Another occasion that literally gave goosebumps to the audience was when the Flyers of 2010 accomplished the "impossible" by winning a playoff series despite falling behind three games to one.

19. Now, this is what we call the most remarkable comeback in the history of the NHL: when Gretzky's Oilers mounted an incredible comeback of 5-0 in 1982.

20. In the Stanley Cup Finals in 1942, the Leafs were behind 3-0 in the series but came storming back to win.

21. The 2014 Kings demonstrated tenacity by overturning a 3-0 deficit to win the Stanley Cup in the series.

22. In 2012, the Boston Bruins and Toronto Maple Leafs played an intense match; the Leafs stayed behind for a while and then marked the winning by 4-1.

23. The Canadiens fell behind 5-1 in 1971, but they used more of their magic to win 7-5. Fans were in shock at what they saw.

24. Imagine a scenario where a team trailing 4-1 in the third period unexpectedly raises the Cup. The Penguins of 1991 accomplished that.

25. The 2013 Blackhawks scored twice in a breathtaking 17-second comeback to win the Stanley Cup.

26. After dropping behind 3-2 in the series, the 2001 Avalanche came back to win the Cup in a thrilling Game 7.

Interesting Hockey Equipment Information

From sharpened and shaped tree branches to a professional, high resin composition, hockey sticks have traveled a long way. No stick can beat the power of today's professional hockey. Do you know that the hockey puck was initially made from cow dung (Kessiby, 2023)?—undoubtedly a great concern for economists and a far-from-hygienic choice. Now, it has been upgraded to synthetic rubber. So come with me, and I'll show you the different transitions in hockey equipment over the past few centuries.

27. Lacrosse balls were once used by hockey players, but because of their strange materials and shapes, they were challenging to use on the ice.

28. Hockey pucks were square in the 19th century, and for flat surfaces, rubber balls had their tops and bottoms removed.

29. Pucks from the early 20th century had layers, but they broke quickly. Vulcanization is the process used to create the durable synthetic rubber used to make pucks nowadays (Kessiby, 2023).

30. In the 1900s, hockey sticks were carved by hand from a single piece of wood, mainly in Mi'kmaq communities in Nova Scotia.

31. Goalie sticks widened by 1930 to allow for faster play. These days, solid and lightweight materials like metal and carbon fiber are used to make hockey sticks (Kessiby, 2023).

32. Goalies' masks were not always a thing; you would be amazed to hear that goalies blocked goals with their faces back in time.

33. In 1979, helmets were made compulsory for NHL players, providing them with an additional layer of protection and a superhero look.

34. Did you ever notice that goalie mask designs are akin to Ironman emblems, showcasing the individuality and sense of style of the netminder?

35. The composite sticks are made of high-tech materials, which improve the player's shot power and accuracy.

36. Goalie gloves have advanced from simple leather to cutting-edge models.

37. Hockey jerseys are more than just outfits; they represent a team's colors with pride and bring players together for a shared goal, much like superhero capes.

Hockey Around the World

Okay, now who thought that hockey was a game played only in Canada? No, my friend, hockey has traveled all around the world with different versions, unlike ice hockey. It is an international sport, not just something played in a specific region! Imagine thrilling ice battles between Sweden and Russia. Places like Finland and the Czech Republic are where hockey players showcase their unique skills.

Even in unlikely countries like the UAE, despite the desert climate, and China, hockey is on the rise! Canada's national sport is hockey, and people are pretty enthusiastic about it. In other words, it's like a giant, awesome party where everyone enjoys skating and scoring goals on ice grounds or artificial hockey fields, regardless of where they're from. Want to catch some juicy facts about hockey's travelogues around the world? Then, hop up with me!

38. Did you know that in the late 19th century, hockey made its way from North America to Europe?

39. International hockey was dominated by the Soviet Union, which displayed its style and flair in storied matches against North American teams.

40. European hockey leagues have their own distinct styles and magical plays.

41. Australia, the land of kangaroos, is home to a flourishing ice hockey scene as well.

42. Canada has won the most gold medals in men's ice hockey at the Winter Olympics, with a total of 9 golds as of 2022.

43. Another great place for hockey fans to go is Japan. Imagine cherry blossoms and slap shots— a combo that's uniquely Japanese.

44. The World Championships are like the Olympics in hockey, where each team gives its best for supremacy on the ice.

45. Hockey has its royal court in India, the land of cricket royalty. The hockey stick and the cricket bat are engaged in a magical battle.

46. Sweden, the Vikings' territory, has some solid hockey players who have won many hockey battles all around the world.

47. With its extensive hockey history, the Czech Republic is like a treasure trove of unforgettable moments and legendary players.

48. Hockey is now a truly global phenomenon, spoken and enjoyed in nations like China. It has indeed become a global language.

Skating Science: Gliding Through Ice Physics!

Ice skating or ice hockey might seem fascinating to you, but these are harder to perform. There is a whole science behind ice skating, and classical mechanics are applied while players are performing on an ice hockey field. Ice skates glide across the ice with ease. Forces on skates go sideways. Fast skaters slide a long way on a single stride before stepping on another. When making a quick start, you are doing short , explosive steps, and when you are already skating fast, your steps and slides are getting longer. Let's look at some science-based skating facts below:

49. Hockey players use the science of friction to glide across the ice with the flexibility of physics maestros. It resembles a physics-based magical dance!

50. Zamboni is used to smooth out the rink to create a perfect playing surface, which is the job of the ice-resurfacing wizard. This keeps the ice ground in top-notch condition.

51. Hockey stops are like controlled chaos. Gamers can abruptly stop using friction, leaving rivals and the laws of physics behind.

52. Skate blades spread a thin layer of water to minimize friction and facilitate a smoother and swifter glide.

53. When the puck is shot, it experiences the Magnus effect, which causes it to curve in the air like a magical spell and surprise goalies and audiences.

54. Due to the centrifugal force, players spin like figure skaters with sticks and pucks in hockey.

55. Another fun fact is that you need those geometry classes for hockey, as goalies use angles and geometry to deflect shots and break the rules of scoring.

56. Ice temperature matters a lot! The colder the ice, the harder the surface will be, and puck movements will be quicker and more unpredictable.

57. Every goal celebration is made more magical by the thunderous atmosphere created by hockey arenas that are built to amplify sound.

58. The power of a slapshot is like a physics explosion, combining the perfect blend of force, angle, and precision.

Incredible Hockey Women

Now it's time to shed light on the fierce, fearless, and fabulous women who made history through their incredible game in the world of hockey. When girls rule on the ice, they do it with style, passion, and a little glitter. Let's catch some fun facts about women in hockey.

59. Women's hockey made its first appearance in the Winter Olympics in 1998.

60. Marie-Philip Poulin made her name in hockey history by doing the "golden goal" in the 2014 Olympics.

61. For women's hockey, the NWHL and CWHL function as superhero leagues, giving players a stage on which to display their abilities.

62. Hockey legend Hayley Wickenheiser proved that talent knows no gender restrictions by playing in men's professional leagues.

63. Women's hockey combines skill, grace, and determination to create an exciting spectacle on the ice, much like a magical potion.

64. By participating in an NHL exhibition game, goaltending pioneer Manon Rhéaume broke through glass ceilings and paved the path for future stars.

65. Like capes, women's hockey jerseys are worn with pride as representations of tenacity and solidarity in the face of adversity.

66. Frequently referred to as the "Wayne Gretzky of women's hockey," Angela James's skill set served as an inspiration to a new generation of players.

67. Women's hockey player Colleen Coyne invented the "spoon curve," a widely recognized curve on sticks, and proved that gender is not a barrier to innovation.

68. Women's hockey is a worldwide phenomenon, with teams and players drawing crowds with their skill on the ice.

Amazing Hockey Instructors

If you think that you can master the art of any sport, skill, or profession without a coach or teacher, then you need to reshape your thoughts. There is always a mastermind behind every successful play, and we call them "coach." Let's peek inside the lies and struggles of some great hockey coaches.

69. In the hockey world, coaches act as the players' enchanted mentors and guides, much like Dumbledore to Harry Potter.

70. With nine Stanley Cup wins under his belt, Scotty Bowman is the Gandalf of coaching—a wise man with a talent for winning championships.

71. Legendary coach Toe Blake is an authentic hockey spell caster, having guided the Canadiens to eight titles.

72. Using "line combinations" as a kind of spell book, coaches combine the ideal players to produce magical moments on the ice.

73. The experiences, foresight, and wisdom of coaches are their strategy boards, which they use to sketch plays that wiggle past defenses like intrigued spells.

74. Herb Brooks was a hockey Merlin who altered an underdog team into gold medal winners at the Olympics, creating the "Miracle on Ice."

75. Paul Maurice, who started his coaching career with the Hartford Whalers at just the age of 28, knows how to bring the best out of his team every time.

Kindness, Gratitude, and Generosity

They say if you have the choice to be anything in this world, be kind, and that sums up why generosity, kindness, and gratefulness are essential traits in the sports field. In team sports, gratitude promotes better interpersonal relationships. Grateful players are fantastic leaders and teammates who get more enjoyment out of the game and stay mentally tough, lowering the likelihood of burnout. Let's take a look at some fun facts below.

76. Darryl Sutter had a knack for in-game adjustments in his coaching career.

77. The "Hockey Fights Cancer" movement raises money and awareness to take on real-life villains, much like a superhero team-up.

78. Players show that superheroes wear skates and jerseys by frequently donating their time and money to charities.

79. A charming custom known as the "teddy bear toss" involves spectators tossing teddy bears onto the ice to create a generous winter wonderland.

80. Hockey teams frequently make hospital visits to children's hospitals, transforming the rooms into happy and encouraging locker rooms.

81. "Hockey is for Everyone" is like a chant that shows everyone is welcome at the rink despite any differences.

82. As a show of sportsmanship, players exchange jerseys with one another after games, turning rivals into friends off the ice.

83. If a player is somehow injured during the game, the opponents all gather up to help them.

84. Hockey communities are like enchanted places; they come together in times of need and demonstrate that the true power play is kindness.

85. The Hockey Hall of Fame is a memorial solely dedicated to players who have marked history in the game.

86. After every game, the "three stars" tradition honors exceptional players, spreading appreciation like stars in the hockey sky.

87. The Lady Byng Memorial Trophy, formerly known as the Lady Byng Trophy, is presented each year to the National Hockey League player who has demonstrated the best type of sportsmanship and gentlemanly conduct combined with a high level of playing ability.

88. The Lady Byng Memorial Trophy has been awarded 89 times.

Part II

Hockey Harmony: Slang, Legends, Superstitions, and Triumphs

Every sport has its own unique language or style of expression, just as every person has a different love language. Do you want to know all the secret codes of that ice rink? Then what are you waiting for? Join me in this unique adventure. Imagine all the hockey players are incredible secret agents, and the game is a world of secret codes. Let's crack these codes with fun hockey terms and slang!

Hockey Vocabulary

89. When the puck hits the crossbar and goes straight into the net, it is called "bar down."

90. "Hat trick" in hockey means scoring three consecutive goals in the game.

91. The space between the goalie's legs is called "five-hole."

92. The player who is tough and loves a good hockey scrap is called a "goon."

93. When the team has an advantage on the field, it's called "power play."

94. The machine that cleans the ice in the meantime breaks is called "Zamboni." Don't worry, it may sound like a monster, but it's not.

95. When a player tricks their opponent with some fancy moves to make them dizzy and lose, it's called "dangler."

96. "Biscuit in the basket" means making the puck rest in the net by scoring a goal. No cookies, sorry.

97. The friendly banter between players on the ice is called "chirping."

98. The act of celebration between the players after scoring a goal is called "celly."

99. The penalty box that is made for the players who misbehave in the game is called the "sin bin."

100. The hockey stick is called "twig."

101. The fans, usually female, who love to watch hockey and have some favorite players are called "puck bunnies."

102. The team that possesses the puck is called "blue sweaters."

The Best Goalies Ever

Just like the guardians of the galaxy, goalies are the superheroes of ice who protect the goal of the opponent from scoring. Many great goaltenders have existed in history, and pinning down all of them is tough. But at least we can give tribute to some of the exceptional names.

103. The goaltender who goes by the name "Dominator" is "Dominik Hasek". He was famous for his unconventional style of acrobatic saves. He led the Czech Republic to a gold medal in the 1998 Olympics.

104. Patrick Roy was a four-time Stanley Cup champion known for his clutch performances in the playoffs.

105. The all-time leader in shutouts and wins in the NHL was Martin Brodeur. He led the New Jersey Devils to 3 Stanley Cup championships.

106. Jacques Ponte was the first goaltender who wore the goalie mask regularly. He also won multiple Stanley Cups.

107. Terry Sawchuk had an incredible record of 103 shutouts, and he was the stalwart for several NHL teams. He was also a four-time winner of the Vezina Trophy.

108. The outstanding goalie Ken Dryden had a relatively short career, but he still committed to the Montreal Canadiens for six Stanley Cups in eight seasons. He was also famous for his calm and composed style.

109. Glenn Hall, who got the nickname "Mr. Goalie," played an incredible 502 consecutive games without a mask.

110. A vital part of the New York Islanders dynasty in the early 1980s, Billy Smith was known for his aggressive style and clutch playoff performances (Kurtzberg, 2012). His unique style earned him the nickname "Battlin' Billy."

111. Ed Belfour, known by his nickname "Eddie the Eagle," won the Vezina Trophy twice and was a vital member of the Dallas Stars 1999 Stanley Cup-winning team.

112. Tony Esposito was a two-time winner of the Vezina Trophy. He was an exceptional player for the Chicago Blackhawks. His butterfly technique had an impact on modern-day goaltending.

Shining Defensemen

Defensemen are the mighty shields of the team who guard the goalie and make strategic plays. These are the superheroes of the team who prevent the opponents from scoring goals. Let's find out some fun facts about the dominating defensemen.

113. Bobby Orr was one of the most outstanding defensemen in the history of hockey because he revolutionized the position with his extreme prowess. He won eight Norris trophies and several other awards. He is known to be the only defenseman to win the league scoring title.

114. Nicklas Lidström was famous for his intelligence on the field and got some exceptional defensive skills. He won seven Norris trophies and played a vital role in the success of the Red Wings.

115. The "blue line" is where the defensemen work out their defensive strategy.

116. Some defensemen have an aptitude for setting up scoring plays, giving them the title of "quarterbacks" on the ice. They are capable of doing some awesome slap shots.

117. Ray Bourque was an iconic defenseman for the Boston Bruins and a five-time winner of the Norris Trophy. Known for his leadership qualities, scoring talent, and durability, he participated in 1,612 regular-season games, the most of any defenseman in NHL history.

118. Doug Harvey was also a seven-time Norris Trophy winner and is regarded as one of the best defensemen of the pre-expansion era. He played a fundamental role in the Montreal Canadiens' dynastic years.

119. The captain of the New York Islanders during their early 1980s dynasty, Denis Potvin, is a three-time Norris Trophy winner and four-time Stanley Cup champion.

120. Chris Pronger was a strong and skilled defenseman who was awarded the Norris Trophy. He was the main hero in helping several teams, such as the St. Louis Blues and Anaheim Ducks, make significant playoff runs.

121. Scott Niedermayer played a crucial role in several Stanley Cup victories, notably those with the New Jersey Devils and Anaheim Ducks.

Sharp Centers

Centers in hockey are as crucial as the queen in the chess game. They can make or break the deal of the game, as they are the playmakers who create magical passes and score epic goals. Let's learn about these hockey technicians.

122. Wayne Gretzky was famous as "The Great One" because he holds many scoring records.

123. When there is a puck drop in a dual and centers are fighting for control, this condition is called "face-off."

124. The epic moment in hockey history was when Mario Lemieux once scored a goal in every possible way: PowerPlay, even-straight, penalty shot, shorthanded, and an empty netter.

125. Sydney Crosby was a well-known center who once played with a broken jaw and proved that centers are tough warriors on the field.

126. Captains wear "C" on their jerseys to symbolize the leader and captain of the team.

127. The "spin-o-rama" is a famous move in hockey where a player spins around while controlling the puck.

128. Centers are excellent at deking opponents and tricking them with slick stick-handling moves.

129. Wayne Gretzky's famous line, "You miss 100% of the shots you don't take," encourages centers to take risks and score goals.

130. To identify open teammates and create scoring opportunities, centers must possess an acute sense of vision.

131. Hockey arenas frequently host incredible face-off circle duels where centers show off their skills in this tactical struggle.

132. The center is the team's strategic mind due to their ability to read the game and make immediate decisions.

133. Some centers are renowned for their skill in the shootout when they go one-on-one with the goalie.

134. The center is the team's multipurpose hero because of their ability to score goals and be playmakers.

135. The captain's duty extends beyond the rink; they frequently represent the team in interviews and serve as a link with coaches and officials.

Fierce Wingers

The most erratic players are the wings, zigzagging between defenses and catching goalies off guard. Lace up your imaginary speed skates, and let's zoom into some facts about the wildest wingers!

136. The quickest and sharpest players in the team fall under the winger's category.

137. They got some fancy moves that blank the opponents.

138. Maurice Richard was famous for his fiery style on the pitch and earned the nickname "Rocket."

139. They use their speed to create breakaway moments and thrill the crowd with one-on-one battles with goalies.

140. The famous golden-haired winger was Bobby Hull, who was given the nickname "Golden Jet" for his blazing speed.

141. They are the snipers who aim for the top corners of the net.

142. Wingers put the puck in the net where goalies cannot reach.

143. Some of them have their own signature celebration styles that make them unique and memorable among fans.

144. They work in tandem with centers and score points.

145. The famous "Russian rocket" winger was Pavel Bure, who was one of the fastest among all.

146. Wingers have the skills to slice through confined spaces with ease to open up scoring opportunities. They frequently play along the boards.

147. Certain wingers have a reputation for playing physically and giving opponents vigorous body checks.

148. The "Breakaway Challenge" in All-Star games is a creative way for wingers to show off their skills and score in style.

Senseless Superstitions

Superstitions are not limited to your household, such as when your grandma would say, "Don't show a baby the mirror, or else they will have delayed teething." They are everywhere, no matter where you go, but I bet you won't be ready for hockey superstitions. So, let's peek inside this mysterious world and find which ones are myths and which ones are facts.

149. Players assume that growing "playoff beards" is a lucky charm.

150. Some players like to touch the goalpost before each game and think they are creating some goalie magic spell.

151. Wayne Gretzky used to tap his stick in the locker room before every game.

152. Some players believe that eating specific meals bring them luck and health for their game.

153. Socks, jerseys, and kit numbers are considered to have unique luck.

154. Some players think that touching the Stanley Cup before winning will jinx their chances.

155. Many players consider tokens or unique coins as their lucky charms and keep them in their gear bags.

156. A few players follow rituals, such as warming up with a different technique or composing their calm through music.

157. The pregame ceremony is infused with a hint of superstition, as many players perform particular routines while the national anthem plays.

158. Certain goalies reserve their steps for the ice and will not cross the blue lines en route to the net.

Overcoming Obstacles

Hockey players do face challenges, from battling through tough losses to career-threatening injuries. No matter what, these players always show true game spirit on the field. Let me take you on an inspirational trip where you will learn the tales of resilience and how these hockey players turned adversity into triumph.

159. Mario Lemieux was battling cancer, but still, it didn't stop his passion for the game.

160. In the Stanley Cup final of 1964, Bobby Baun scored a winning goal with a broken leg.

161. Saku Koivu returned to the ground to continue his career after fighting and beating cancer.

162. Jaromir Jagr proved that age is just a number and continued to excel on the hockey field well into his 40s.

163. Multiple injuries couldn't stop the legend, Cam Neely, from coming back to the ground.

164. Despite facing serious concussion challenges, Paul Kariya displayed his skills and abilities by returning to the game.

165. Patrice Bergeron led his team to success in the Stanley Cup Final despite playing with a punctured lung.

166. Gordie Howe also proved that age doesn't matter when it comes to pursuing your passion. He retired for a brief time and then returned to the NHL.

167. One of the G.O.A.T goaltenders in the history of hockey, Dominic Hasek, started his NHL career at a later age.

168. Despite being instructed at the age of 18 not to play hockey, Zdeno Chara bucked the odds and became a legend.

169. Throughout his career, Nicklas Lidström displayed incredible consistency and competence, earning the nickname "The Perfect Human.

170. Following heart surgery, Henrik Lundqvist made a comeback on the ice, proving his unrelenting drive and enthusiasm for the sport.

171. Regardless of difficulties and setbacks, Steve Yzerman led his team with courage and determination.

172. After overcoming a career-threatening injury, Max Pacioretty became a leader and an important member of his team.

173. Early in his career, Brett Hull encountered critics, but he went on to become one of the NHL's all-time top goal scorers.

Outstanding Friendships

Hockey isn't just about goals and victories. It also has multiple details of fan stories and incredible friendships, making the game even more special. Let's shed light on meeting favorite players and sharing unforgettable moments with fellow fans.

174. Two kids from separate locations who shared a love of hockey became pen buddies because of their mutual admiration for the Toronto Maple Leafs.

175. A group of fans met at a Toronto Maple Leafs hockey game and discovered that they live in the same area; now, they attend every game together and have a close relationship.

176. A grandfather, his son, and grandson have a particular affinity with their beloved club, the Chicago Blackhawks, and have attended every game together for years.

177. A young fan's wish came true when their favorite New York Rangers player paid a surprise visit on their birthday. The athlete not only signed his autograph but also took the young fan skating.

178. Two Montreal Canadiens fans met during a hockey game, fell in love, and married in a hockey-themed wedding.

179. Fans from all over the world join online discussions to express their views, opinions, and passion for the game, particularly their favorite team, the Pittsburgh Penguins.

180. A group of guys, all Edmonton Oilers fans, agreed to take a cross-country road trip to see every game of their team's playoff season.

181. Some hockey players, such as those from the Calgary Flames, paid visits to young fans in hospitals who were facing different medical conditions, making it the most memorable day of their lives.

182. At a Vancouver Canucks game, a fan who couldn't afford the tickets received a surprise ticket from a fellow fan described as a "ticket fairy."

183. A group of Vegas Golden Knights fans established a tradition of ordering pizza after each home game victory. What began as a simple celebration evolved into a cherished custom that deepened their friendship.

Part III

Hockey Marvels: Fun, Legends, and Mascot Magic

You will always need more of this game, no matter how dense the information you collect. It's like the onion layers: the more you peel, the more layers will emerge from within. As Jarome Iginla once said, "Each goal, each win, going to different buildings, the rivalries, the excitement—it is something. I try to catch myself, you know, in the warm-ups, when you're on the line and the anthem, and you get to some milestones and stuff. It's such a neat experience."

So let's explore what has been hidden from your sights till now, young players!

Bendy Rules

Once in our lifetime, we all want to break or amend some rules and do what our hearts say, don't you agree? And you will be surprised to hear that in the world of hockey, rules do get a little bent. It's like a cartoon where the characters find creative ways to score goals. Let's dig deeper into some crazy rule-bending facts about hockey.

185. In the NHL All-Star game of 1979, the players scored 19 goals in the third period because the scoreboard malfunctioned.

186. Ron Hextall became the first hockey goalie to shoot and secure a goal in a regular-season game.

187. The "flying V" formation, made famous by the Mighty Ducks in the movies, was attempted in real life and in NHL games, too.

188. In 1974, the fans of the Buffalo Sabres threw so many souvenir pugs onto the field that the game had to be postponed.

189. In 1979, the Hartford Whalers' coach dressed up as his team's mascot to inspire his players.

190. Gillies Gratton claimed that his performance was better than the stars aligned, and the moon was in the right phase.

191. Goalie Jacques Plante started the trend of goalies wearing masks in 1953. It was against the rules at first, but he bent them, and now all the goalies wear one.

192. The "spin-o-rama" move was so good that they had to create a role just for it.

193. Wayne Gretzky, the famous hockey legend, used to miss the net intentionally, which made his opponents think that he had poor aim.

194. In the 1970s, Don Saleski scored a goal with his skate; it was allowed because he didn't kick it intentionally.

195. The Zamboni of the New York Islanders was a unique float in their 1980 victory parade.

196. The 1980s Edmonton Oilers dynasty was about more than just hockey. In a Saturday morning cartoon called "ProStars," Wayne Gretzky co-starred with Michael Jordan and Bo Jackson!

197. The Vancouver Canucks created hockey fashion history in 1977 when they became the first team to wear black skate blades, giving their uniform a sleek new look.

198. In the early days of hockey, players could use any stick they pleased, including those with blades bent like a banana! It was not until later that guidelines were established to standardize stick shapes.

199. Before forward passes were permitted, players had to carry the puck up the rink themselves. When the rule was finally implemented in 1929, it significantly altered the game, resulting in faster-paced and more strategic gameplay.

200. The NHL implemented the "Gretzky Rule" in 1979, which limited the number of players who may serve as leaders or alternative captains on a team.

201. This was in response to the Edmonton Oilers using many players with the "C" or "A" to confound opponents.

Hockey and Culture Through Art

Hockey is more than just goals and pucks. It serves as a blank canvas for artistic expression as well. Jon Rye once proudly said, "The Art of Hockey competition celebrates the start of our journey as a museum into the world of education." Let's explore the artistic elements that transform hockey from a mere sport into a vibrant cultural masterpiece, from eye-catching team logos to the rhythmic sounds of skaters on ice!

202. The Zamboni can create mesmerizing patterns on the ice.

203. Teams choose cool mascots and logos, such as the Detroit Red Wings logo, which looks like a wheel with wings.

204. The logo of the Montréal Canadiens features an H with a C inside.

205. The spirit of the game is often showcased by beautiful paintings and murals displayed on ice rinks.

206. Some players are famous for their signature moves, which make the game more entertaining.

207. Each team has a unique hockey jersey that displays its colors, history, and culture.

208. The sound of skates cutting through the ice is like a rhythmic beat.

209. Players have different styles of celebrating their goals, which is also an art form.

210. The Boston Garden's Green Monster is one of the arena's famous features that give the hockey experience even more character and charm.

211. The Stanley Cup is a work of art created by expert craftspeople, not just a trophy. It even has the cup keeper as its protector!

212. Hockey pucks are kept frozen until needed.

213. Throwing an octopus on the field has been considered lucky since 1952.

214. The Mighty Ducks were named after a Disney movie in 2007.

215. Players use the Stanley Cup as a snack bowl after winning.

216. If the goalies of both teams are injured somehow, anyone from the audience or the fans can be the backup goalie.

Hockey in the Years to Come

Alright, little palmists, what do you think about the future of hockey? How would it feel if hockey were to be played in the air like a quidditch match, say in 2050? Let's explore the future of hockey together, where talent, technology, skills, and fun come in a package.

217. Sensor-equipped smart jerseys may soon be able to track players' movements.

218. Training in virtual reality is growing in prominence. Visualize improving your slap shot without ever setting foot on the ice!

219. Drones could record breathtaking aerial footage of hockey games.

220. Goalie-training robots could assist players in perfecting their game.

221. Hockey equipment that has been 3D printed may be precisely tailored to each player, guaranteeing a tight fit for maximum comfort and performance.

222. Sensor-equipped hockey sticks could evaluate passes and shots, giving players immediate feedback to help them improve.

223. During a game, augmented reality glasses could display player information and statistics directly to you.

224. Interactive holograms during games could be a feature of future arenas.

225. Research on climate-friendly ice rinks is underway.

226. Social media could enable virtual meet-and-greets and behind-the-scenes peeks, bringing fans and their favorite players closer together.

227. Smart helmets and other wearable technology can give players real-time data on their performance, which could help them improve their skills.

228. Coaches can use high-speed cameras to help with strategic analysis and player growth by capturing the exact details of the players' movements.

229. Biometric tracking devices could keep an eye on the players' health and levels of fatigue to guarantee peak performance and avoid injuries.

230. Sensr-equipped smart pucks could completely change the way players play by giving them instant access to data on goal-line technology, impact, and speed.

231. Ice technology advancements could include surfaces that control temperature, produce optimal playing conditions, and require less ice maintenance.

Unheralded Bench Greats

In the game of hockey, not everyone is a player, but some of them are the great pillars on whom these amazing players rely. They are the unsung heroes of the game, working their magic from the bench. Let's have a look at these great and pure souls.

232. The water bottle guys keep the players hydrated.

233. The equipment managers make it possible for the payers to have just the right gear they need.

234. The trainers use their skills, information, and education to heal the injuries of the players and make them fit again.

235. The coaches are the real puppet hamsters behind the show.

236. Cheerleaders hype up the passion and excitement of the crowd.

237. The guy waving the towels keeps the bench spotless and the players sweat-free.

238. Backup goalies wait patiently for their turn, prepared to guard the net if the starting goalie needs a break.

239. Scouts search the world for untapped talent in order to identify future stars.

240. Team doctors protect athletes from game-related bumps and ensure their continued health.

241. The mascot makes fans happy and laugh, transforming the arena into a fun-filled playground.

242. The ice crew members maintain the rink for a successful play.

243. Player statistics are monitored by the statistician, converting the game into a mathematical playground.

244. With their loud voices, public address announcers raise the stakes, turning every goal announcement into a moment of pure hockey drama.

245. Stunt coordinators transform mascots into daredevils by organizing exciting on-ice performances.

246. Costume designers provide mascots with colorful costumes to make them lively representatives of their teams.

Historic Hockey Events

Have you ever had such a wonderful moment in your life that stays rent-free in your mind? Well, hockey has many such great moments that you sure want to relive. Let's have a look at them.

247. Wayne Gretzky scored 50 goals in 39 games—a true legend for a reason.

248. The 1980 "Miracle on Ice" saw the Soviet Union's strong team defeated by the U.S. team, setting up an iconic Olympic moment.

249. Etched in hockey history is Bobby Orr's iconic flying goal from 1970, in which he skyrocketed through the air following his Stanley Cup-winning goal.

250. In 1936, the NHL played its longest game ever—six overtime periods.

251. In 1988, Mario Lemieux scored a crazy goal where he played hockey magic, slicing through the entire opposition team.

252. As the first player to score 50 goals in a single season, Maurice "Rocket" Richard established a benchmark for goal-scoring greats in the future.

253. The Buffalo Sabres and Philadelphia Flyers played in dense fog during the "fog game" in 1975, which produced a mysterious and intriguing atmosphere.

254. A player who gets into a fight in a game, scores, and notches an assist in the same game is called a "Gordie Howe hat trick." It's a rare and legendary feat.

255. A goal from the 1992 Stanley Cup Finals is known as the "no goal" because it was controversially disallowed, sparking discussions that are still remembered in hockey history.

256. Sidney Crosby's "golden goal" in the 2010 Winter Olympics helped Canada win on home ice and cemented his legacy in Canadian hockey history.

257. Hasek's "greatest save" came during a playoff game between the Sabres and Devils in 1994.

258. In 1917, the NHL began uniting pro teams under one league, laying the foundation for today's NHL and iconic rivalries.

259. One of the most celebrated goals in history was when Alex Ovechkin scored "the goal" against the Phoenix Coyotes in 2006.

260. Darryl Sutter set a new NHL record in 1976 for maximum points in one game by scoring six goals and helping four others.

261. In 1988, Mario Lemieux set a record by scoring five goals in five different styles in a single game.

Hockey's Women Pioneers

The ice ring was not always a place for everyone, but thanks to the incredible pioneers of women's hockey, the barriers melted away. Now, girls can finally lace up their skates and join the action. Let's take a peek inside the great female players' success stories that broke the ice.

262. The Canadian hockey icon Hayley Wickenheiser played in the men's professional league.

263. The first Women's World Championship took place in 1990 and showcased top-tier talent on the international platform (Njororai, 2014).

264. Manon Rhéaume was the first woman to play as a goalie in an NHL game in 1992 (Bertovich, 2019).

265. To give female players access to professional opportunities, the Professional Women's Hockey Players Association (PWHPA) and the National Women's Hockey League (NWHL) were established in 2015.

266. Due to the dominance of schools like the University of Minnesota, women's college hockey in the United States has grown to be a major sport.

267. Women's hockey has greatly benefited from the Winter Olympics, raising global awareness of the sport's talent and competitiveness.

268. Often referred to as the Wayne Gretzky of women's hockey, Angela James was a trailblazer in the sport and was a significant player in taking women's hockey to new heights.

269. Since its introduction in 2009, Canada's top championship trophy for women's professional hockey is the Clarkson Cup.

270. Women's hockey's entry into the Winter Paralympics has given athletes with disabilities a platform to display their amazing abilities.

271. Women's ice hockey became an official Olympic sport for the first time at the Nagano Olympics in 1998, providing opportunities for female athletes around the globe.

272. In 2022, Kelsey Koelzer became the first female referee in NHL playoff history, breaking down barriers and opening the door for greater female representation in hockey.

273. At the 2014 and 2018 Winter Olympics, Canadian hockey player Marie-Philip Poulin created history by scoring the goal that won the gold medal.

274. The IIHF decided to increase the physicality of the game by implementing body checking in women's ice hockey at the U18 level in 2023.

275. American hockey sensation Hilary Knight demonstrated her scoring ability by becoming the IIHF Women's World Championship's all-time top scorer.

276. With the launch of the Global Girls' Game in 2019, female players from all over the world were brought together to strengthen their friendships and advance the sport of women's hockey.

Hockey Through the Seasons

Who says that hockey is just a winter wonderland spectacle? Keep your ears from such thoughts; hockey is as much a summer street play as it is an ice rink game. This sport goes all year long, no matter the location or season. Let's disclose some fun facts about four-seasoned hockey.

277. In the summer, street hockey players trade in their skates for sneakers and transform parks and driveways into makeshift arenas.

278. Top teams from across the world come together to compete in the IIHF World Championship, which heats up the ice in the spring.

279. During the warm months, roller hockey players can zip around on wheels as they take the game to the streets.

280. For hockey fans, the June NHL Awards are a highlight of the summer as they honor the best players of the campaign.

281. The NHL season begins in the fall, and fans can't wait for their favorite teams to return.

282. Played on New Year's Day in outdoor stadiums, the Winter Classic blends the magic of the season with hockey.

283. Played on frozen lakes, pond hockey combines natural beauty with a hint of nostalgia.

284. The IIHF U18 World Championship highlights the skills of young players and gives a glimpse into the sport's future stars.

285. International hockey competition is made more festive by the Spengler Cup, which is held in Switzerland during the holidays.

286. In January, the NHL All-Star Weekend brings excitement to the winter blues with dazzling skills competitions and a star-studded game.

287. Street hockey tournaments, such as the NHL Street Tour, bring communities together in the spirit of the game by converting neighborhoods into vibrant arenas.

288. An annual feature of the sport is the World Outdoor Ball Hockey Championship, where players showcase their prowess on outdoor rinks.

289. Played on smooth surfaces with rollerblades, inline hockey leagues offer enthusiasts a summertime alternative that combines skill and speed.

290. Held in conjunction with the All-Star Weekend, the NHL Fan Fair transforms into a winter wonderland for hockey enthusiasts by inviting fans to participate in interactive exhibits.

291. With NHL players serving as instructors, summer hockey camps give budding players the opportunity to improve their abilities and spread their passion for the sport to their heroes.

Hockey's Animal Kingdom

Okay, so, my little smart buddies, did you know that hockey teams have their furry friends like you do? Well, hockey animals are a bit different from your cat, which has a bottle-brush tail. They have mascots who bring laughter, joy, and a whole lot of entertainment to the game. Let's find out which team has what mascot.

292. The mascot of the Philadelphia Flyers, Gritty, is well-known for his outrageous antics and quirky charm.

293. Mascots may switch teams, as shown by Youppi!, the former mascot of the Montreal Expos, who now plays for the Montreal Canadiens!

294. The Tampa Bay Lightning's mascot, Thunderbug, is modeled after an insect and zips around the arena, adding excitement and exhilaration to Lightning games.

295. The lion mascot for the LA Kings, Bailey, is a delightful crowd-pleaser who enjoys dancing and entertaining fans.

296. During games, the Minnesota Wild's adorable lynx, Nordy, plays playful antics that highlight the team's wild side.

297. The Buffalo Sabres' saber-toothed tiger, Sabretooth, brings a little dinosaur fun to the game of hockey.

298. The Columbus Blue Jackets' bug mascot, Stinger, buzzes around the rink, bringing joy and happiness.

299. During games, Iceburgh, the penguin representing the Pittsburgh Penguins, charms fans with his cutesy antics.

300. The wolf mascot of the Arizona Coyotes, Howler, howls with excitement and livens up the desert hockey scene.

301. The bear mascot of the Boston Bruins, Blades, is a traditional figure with a playful side who delights fans with his antics.

302. The mascot of the St. Louis Blues, Louie, is the groovy representative of Blues Country, as he skates into hearts with his smooth moves.

303. The mascot of the Calgary Flames, Harvey the Hound, is well-known for his huge tongue and brings a touch of canine charm to Flames games.

304. The mascot of the New York Islanders, Sparky the Dragon, brings fiery excitement to the arena and is a lively companion to the team.

305. The mascot of the Anaheim Ducks, Wild Wing, takes off with animated antics, demonstrating that ducks can add humor and a fanciful touch to hockey.

306. The Chicago Blackhawks' mascot, Tommy Hawk, is a favorite bird of prey because he combines toughness with a goofy grin.

Part IV

Stars on Ice: Tales of Hockey Heroes, Prodigies, and Legends

The Colors of Hockey

Close your eyes and imagine you are visiting an ancient land with people traveling on horses, getting water from the wells, and watching the direction of the sun to estimate the time and date. Now tell me, what would happen if you simply added some vibrance to those images? It will make the scenario even more beautiful and eye-catching. Similarly, hockey has had its own set of colors over the past few years. So get on this adventure train, as we are going to travel through different hockey styles and their meanings.

307. The iconic Chicago Blackhawks logo has a Native American headdress, which represents strength and bravery.

308. One of the most prominent uniforms in sports history is the red, white, and blue one worn by the Montreal Canadiens.

309. The 1980s "Flying Skate" jersey worn by the Vancouver Canucks is a fan-favorite throwback that adds vintage flair to the rink.

310. The burgundy and blue colors of the Colorado Avalanche honor the team's rocky mountain heritage.

311. The Arizona Coyotes presented a jersey inspired by Kachinas to highlight the team's ties to the desert.

312. The red and white jerseys of the Detroit Red Wings are renowned for their classic, subtle style.

313. The Pittsburgh Penguins honored the city's steel industry by introducing the "Pittsburgh Gold" color.

314. The Los Angeles Kings' 1980s purple and gold jerseys are a vivid throwback to the glam rock era.

315. Hockey fans have both criticized and loved the 1990s New York Islanders fisherman logo jersey.

316. The metallic gold jerseys of the Vegas Golden Knights add a glamorous and glitzy touch to the NHL.

317. The "Buffaslug" jersey of the Buffalo Sabres' divided fans features a stylized buffalo.

318. The orange jerseys worn by the Edmonton Oilers are a tribute to the province's oil industry as well as the team's early 1980s success.

319. Storm warning flags adorn the black alternate jersey of the Carolina Hurricanes, lending an air of danger.

320. On the ice, the Florida Panthers' red, gold, and navy blue colors create a striking and aggressive look.

321. The Minnesota Wild's connection with the state's wilderness is reflected in the team's wheat and forest green jerseys.

Hockey and Technology

Technology is not only used when your teacher presents slides to teach you different science or social lessons. Hockey, too, has a very strong and irreplaceable relationship with technology, just as Dexter has with his laboratory. Come with me, and we will explore some technical hockey facts together.

322. To make sure that the goal decision is correct, goal-line technology uses cameras to detect the movement of the puck.

323. Referees can inspect close calls again with the help of video review, ensuring that the correct calls are made in the rink.

324. With sensors tracking its movement, the "Smart Puck" can provide information on shot speed, distance traveled, and other metrics.

325. Personalized fitness trackers are now used by hockey players to monitor their performance and improve their training.

326. Fans can see hockey games from above with never-before-seen perspectives thanks to drone footage.

327. Robotic goalie trainers help players improve their shooting by simulating real-game situations.

328. Hockey gear can be customized thanks to 3D printing technology, guaranteeing a perfect fit for every player.

329. Players' movements may soon be tracked by smart jerseys with embedded sensors, making the game a high-tech experience.

330. In the near future, the audience can catch a real-time sight of the data and statistics of the players through augmented reality (AR) glasses.

331. Interactive holograms could be added to arenas in the future to give audiences an immersive experience.

332. Climate-friendly ice rinks look into eco-friendly methods to make sure that the fun of hockey doesn't hurt the environment.

333. Social media platforms facilitate virtual meet-and-greets and behind-the-scenes scenarios, allowing fans to get closer to their favorite players.

334. The NHL employs sophisticated analytics and statistics to learn more about team tactics and player performance.

335. Referees can confer on calls thanks to referee communication systems, which guarantee justice on the ice.

Hockey Haunts and Legends

Mysteries are not just limited to Hogwarts; hockey, too, sometimes gets a little mysterious and fishy. Many legendary tales, myths, and assumptions about hockey might surprise you. So take a flashlight, wear your 3D glasses, and walk silently with me through these eerie paths.

336. The ghosts of hockey legends reside in Toronto's Hockey Hall of Fame, preserving their successes.

337. It is said that the "curse of the Stanley Cup" follows teams that win the cup but experience bad luck soon after.

338. Some people think that the ghosts of former Canadian players haunt the Montreal Forum.

339. The "Gretzky curse" proposes that the teams involved in the Wayne Gretzky trade suffered misfortune.

340. Legends of the "Original Six" era are filled with iconic tales and bitter rivalries that echo through time.

341. The legendary "Hockeytown" name belongs to Detroit, celebrating the city's profound connection to the sport.

342. The famous flying goal that Bobby Orr scored in 1970 is immortalized in hockey history and is shown in a statue outside of the T.D. Garden (Brown, 2019).

343. The mysterious "cup keepers" protect the Stanley Cup, maintaining its safety and preserving its storied history.

344. With its captivating ice-resurfacing dance, the Zamboni has turned into a quirky hockey legend.

345. The 1980 Olympics' "Miracle on Ice" saw the underdog U.S. team overcome the powerful Soviet Union, creating a tale for centuries to come (Ryan & Lieser, 2008).

346. Throwing hats on the ice for a player who scores three goals is known as the "hat trick," and it has a colorful and long history.

347. It is said that the "hockey gods" have an impact on games, favoring teams or individuals with extraordinary skill and sportsmanship.

348. Bobby Hull, also popularly known as the "Golden Jet," is renowned for his devastating slap shots and his influence on the game.

349. A legendary moment in hockey history is the 1997 "Brawl in Hockeytown" between the Colorado Avalanche and the Detroit Red Wings (Myers, 2022).

350. A hockey arena's eerie glow at night, with just one spotlight shining on the ice, creates a surreal and mysterious atmosphere.

Epic Hockey Tournaments

When amazing teams from all around the world gather on one platform for glory and lift the coveted trophies, it becomes an extraordinary sports saga. Each tournament has its own set of tales of triumphs, heartbreaks, celebrations, and the pursuit of success. So, are you ready to read some amazing facts about the epic tournaments? Then let's go!

351. The top hockey players from around the world compete at the Winter Olympics, showcasing their skills.

352. National teams come together for the IIHF World Championship, which is a worldwide display of skill and sportsmanship.

353. The top hockey countries come together for the World Cup of Hockey, which adds an exciting twist with a format that goes beyond traditional international play.

354. Dating back to 1923, the Spengler Cup is one of the oldest ice hockey tournaments taking place in Switzerland.

355. The top teams from Canada's major junior leagues compete in the Memorial Cup, a junior hockey championship.

356. Top European hockey teams compete in the annual Karjala Cup, an international competition held in Europe.

357. A combination of national teams and select squads participate in exciting competitions in the Deutschland Cup in Germany.

358. As part of the Euro Hockey Tour, Russia, Sweden, Finland, and the Czech Republic compete against one another in the Channel One Cup.

359. The World Junior Ice Hockey Championship, which showcases top young players from across the world, is a fan favorite.

360. The Ivan Hlinka Memorial Tournament is an under-18 tournament that celebrates and pays tribute to the renowned Czech coach.

361. To promote regional competition, the Asia League Ice Hockey brings together teams from China, South Korea, Japan, and Russia.

362. Young talent is showcased at the World U-17 Hockey Challenge, providing an early look at the sport's future stars.

363. The NHL All-Star Game is an incredible display of skill where the best players in the league display their abilities in celebration of hockey excellence.

364. The College Hockey America (CHA) Tournament, which features intense competitions between college teams, determines the NCAA champions.

365. Top women's teams compete in the Women's World Championship, emphasizing the intensity and skill of women's hockey on a global scale.

Hockey's Hidden Gems

Hockey is not something that you practice to learn in adulthood; it's a talent that you are born with. Lucky are those who recognize their hockey skills from an early age. A tremendous world of talent lies in the junior hockey leagues. These leagues provide ground for the minors to nourish their inner spirit and bring out their best. Let's see what these juniors have shown to the world of hockey.

366. The American Hockey League (AHL) serves as the NHL's main development league, nurturing rising stars before they make their big debut.

367. A premier A.A. league, the ECHL (formerly the East Coast Hockey League), serves as a springboard for players hoping to make it to the AHL and NHL.

368. One of Canada's main junior league systems, the Canadian Hockey League (CHL), produces elite players for the professional ranks.

369. The SPHL (Southern Professional Hockey League) adds a Southern flair to the minor league landscape, with teams participating in the southeastern United States.

370. College hockey is supported by the NCAA (National Collegiate Athletic Association), which also produces a pipeline of talent for the major and minor leagues.

371. A junior league that prepares players not only for college but also for professional hockey careers is the USHL (United States Hockey League).

372. Top talent from Europe and beyond is drawn to the KHL (Kontinental Hockey League), a significant professional league that operates outside of North America.

373. The Swedish Hockey League, or SHL, is a top European league that serves as a springboard for international careers and adds to the worldwide talent pool.

374. The coveted trophy for the league champions is the AHL's Calder Cup, which represents excellence in minor league hockey.

375. Teams fight hard to be the first to lift the coveted Kelly Cup, which is given to the league champions in the ECHL.

376. For Canadian major junior teams, winning the Memorial Cup is the ultimate goal and a symbol of dominance in the CHL.

377. The top college hockey teams in the NCAA compete for the coveted national title in the Frozen Four.

378. The AHL All-Star Classic brings together the league's best players to give up-and-coming players a stage.

379. Teams choose players from minor and other leagues to join them in the NHL Entry Draft in an attempt to fulfill their goal of having an NHL player.

380. In addition to helping coaches and referees improve their craft, the minor leagues also contribute to the general development of hockey.

Hockey and Community Outreach

Hockey is not just a game; it's an emotion that brings communities together; it inspires teamwork, coordination, positive reinforcement, and bonding. This game touches and improves lives and makes a difference in the world.

381. Through the NHL's Hockey Fights Cancer campaign, the hockey community comes together to raise money and awareness for cancer patients.

382. Many NHL teams actively engage in charitable endeavors, such as hospital visits and community clean-ups, exemplifying the giving spirit.

383. The "Hockey Is For Everyone" campaign encourages inclusivity by extending a warm welcome to hockey enthusiasts of all identities, abilities, and backgrounds.

384. Through equipment donations, the NHL players' association's Goals & Dreams fund enables underprivileged kids to enjoy the joys of hockey.

385. The goal of the NHL Green initiative is to promote environmentally sustainable practices within the league and encourage fans to follow suit.

386. The Hockey Fights Hate campaign by the NHL tackles social issues and highlights how hockey can be used to fight injustice and discrimination.

387. The NHL preseason games are hosted in local communities; funds for arena upgrades are awarded as part of the Kraft Hockeyville program, which honors local hockey enthusiasts.

388. Using the passion for hockey to help those in need, the volunteer-based organization, Hockey Helps the Homeless, hosts competitions and other events to generate money for homeless shelters.

389. The NHL Foundation distributes funds to assist underprivileged children and families, improving community development, health, and education.

390. Hockey players frequently visit schools to share their passion for the game with the next generation, encourage physical fitness, and inspire young minds.

391. Through hockey and STEM education, the NHL's Future Goals program introduces students to science, technology, engineering, and math.

392. The Hockey Canada Foundation supports local efforts financially to promote the expansion of hockey at the grassroots level.

393. To honor veterans and active-duty military personnel for their service and sacrifice, NHL teams host military appreciation nights.

394. The "Hockey Across America" initiative highlights the game's influence on communities across the country while honoring its diverse fan base.

395. The goal of the IIHF's Hockey Development Program is to make hockey more accessible and enjoyable for kids around the world.

The Top Five Referees from the World of Hockey

Referees are like the mother of the game. Just as your mom makes you follow the rules in the house, keeps justice among all you siblings, divides everything equally, and keeps an eye on your conduct, a referee in hockey or any game does the same. They are responsible for enforcing the game rules; they are the eyes, ears, and nose of the field and can easily detect if something goes off limits. Referees, who are distinguished by their distinctive black and white stripes, are vital to the game's integrity because they monitor player behavior, goal calls, penalties, and other infractions. As Wayne Gretzky said, "I learned that if you're a high-spirited, enthusiastic referee, you're bound to be a game-changer. The best referees blend fairness, precision, and a love for the sport."

Let's get to know some of the most famous referees in the history of hockey.

Kerry Fraser–The Hockey Hair Guru

So, guys, at number one, meet Kerry Fraser, famous for his cool hockey hair. For 30 years, Kerry zipped around the ice, made calls, and turned several heads every time with new flowing locks. And that's not just it; after stepping out of the rink, he became a hockey analyst and shared his wisdom and entertaining hockey tales with his many fans.

Facts

396. He was lovingly known as "Cujo" after a wild-haired movie character.

397. Kerry was a style icon and rocked the "no helmet" look despite it being prohibited for players.

398. He supervised 1,900 regular-season games as an official.

399. He transitioned into a hockey analyst who brought style to conversations after the games.

400. On the ice, his unique hairstyle and mustache made him instantly identifiable.

Bill McCreary–The Zen Referee

Moving forward to number 2, we have Bill McCreary, also known as the Zen master of refereeing. Without ever losing his cool, he officiated on the ice rink for 28 years with his wonderful skill of fair play justice.

Facts

401. He is renowned for his calm and collected style when skating.

402. He was the first official to oversee 1,700 NHL regular-season games to set a record.

403. He skillfully and gracefully handled multiple Stanley Cup Finals.

404. After hanging up his skates, he actively mentored aspiring referees.

405. He was proficient in interacting with players and managing games.

Don Koharski–The Animated Officiator

Don Koharski, famously known for turning hockey calls into a performance, gave his 32 precious and wisdomful years to hockey. He had a unique energy when he was on ice. He made sure that every call was a spectacle.

Facts

406. He was renowned for his expressive and lively on-ice officiating style.

407. He gained popularity after a coach referred to him as a "fat pig" during a playoff game.

408. He supervised over 1,700 games and many playoffs during the regular season.

409. He evolved into a performing supervisor who mentored the upcoming generation.

410. He was a memorable figure in hockey officiating because of his vibrant personality.

Dan O'Halloran–The Swift Decision Maker

Introducing Dan O'Halloran, the remarkable referee who effortlessly transformed swift decision-making into a true art form! With an impressive 21 seasons in the NHL under his belt, Dan's ability to make quick and precise calls ensured that the game flowed seamlessly.

Facts

411. He was the man for making accurate and immediate decisions on ice.

412. He was also capable of handling stressful situations, having officiated several Stanley Cup Finals.

413. Despite the difficulties of officiating, Dan always kept a cheerful disposition.

414. He made accurate and effective calls that helped the game flow smoothly.

415. He was active in charitable projects, highlighting the advantages of hockey.

Wes McCauley–The Signal Showman

Now comes Wes McCauley, the referee who has raised the art of penalty signals to a whole new level! Coming from a lineage of referees, Wes brings an unparalleled flair and dramatic touch to every call he makes. His unique style turns games into captivating shows that keep fans on the edge of their seats.

Facts

416. This guy is well known for his theatrical and animated penalty signals, which add excitement to every call.

417. He hails from a family of referees, with his father, John, having been an NHL referee; basically, it runs in the family.

418. His unique style adds a fun element to the game and garners cheers from fans.

419. Videos of his penalty signals frequently go viral on social media, making him a fan favorite.

420. A man who gives back, he is actively involved in multiple charitable initiatives.

Some Renowned Hockey Players

So, champs, tell me, which one is your hockey inspiration? How much do you know about your favorite players? Let's peek inside the hockey lives of some legends.

Connor McDavid–The Speed Maestro

Connor McDavid has proved himself to be the speedster of ice at just the age of 25. The man has got a youthful charm along with sleek moves. McDavid embodies the innovative face of the game with his focused gaze and lean build. A living powerhouse, he has the lightning speed to weave through defenses and deliver pinpoint passes. This man leads the Edmonton Oilers with passion, grace, and determination, with a captain's 'C' on his jersey.

Facts

421. At the age of 19, McDavid became the youngest captain in NHL history.

422. He won the Ted Lindsay, Hart, and Art Ross awards in the same season.

423. Currently, McDavid holds the NHL All-Star Skills Competition record for fastest lap.

424. He gave a personal donation of $100,000 to the COVID-19 relief effort.

425. Before joining the NHL, he dominated the OHL while playing for the Erie Otters.

Sidney Crosby–The Maestro on Ice

The young, smart, and talented 34-year-old Sidney Crosby is the uncrowned king on the ice. His style is a perfect mixture of leadership and finesse. He is named "Sid the Kid," and he has an extraordinary vision, a knack for scoring solid goals, and mismatched playmaking skills. The Pittsburgh Penguins won several Stanley Cups under his leadership.

Facts

426. He scored Canada's "Golden Goal" at the Winter Olympics in 2010.

427. Crosby was a gold medalist at the Olympics, World Championship, and Stanley Cup, making him a member of the elite group, The Triple Gold Club.

428. He won the Calder Trophy after being selected first overall in the 2005 draft, living up to the excitement right away.

429. Sid became one of the fastest players in NHL history to reach 1,000 career points in just 757 games.

430. As proof of the league's respect for him, he was chosen several times by his peers as the most outstanding player.

Auston Matthews—The Sniper

The Toronto Maple Leafs sniper is 24-year-old Auston Matthews. Matthews adds a little vintage style to the modern game with his robust build and trademark mustache.

Matthews' deadly scoring prowess defines his style. With a simple flick of the wrist, his dangerously accurate shots can alter the course of the match. Matthews is an important member of the Maple Leafs team, which is leading the Original Six group.

Facts

431. Matthews became the first player to score four goals in his NHL debut in the modern era.

432. He took home the Maurice "Rocket" Richard Trophy after scoring the most goals in the league.

433. He was born in Scottsdale, Arizona, which is unusual for a hockey player.

434. He backs a range of humanitarian projects, including mental health-related ones.

435. As the Maple Leafs' backup captain, he demonstrated leadership abilities.

Alex Ovechkin–The Goal-Scoring Machine

Known by his nickname "The Great Eight," Alex Ovechkin is a seasoned goal-scoring veteran with unmatched powerful shots. He spread smiles on others' faces with his sweet, gap-toothed grin and rugged charms.

Facts

436. This man holds the record for most hat tricks ever by a player born in Russia.

437. He was Rookie of the Year in 2006, delivering results early in his career.

438. This dude also has an aggressive playing style.

439. Ovechkin dominated in goals scored, taking home the esteemed trophy seven times.

440. He led the Washington Capitals in 2018 to their historic Stanley Cup victory.

441. Ovechkin is a relentless player, missing very few games during his career.

Marc-André Fleury–The Smiling Netminder

Marc-André Fleury brings a smile on the face of an intense goaltending position with his friendly demeanor. Fleury is known for his firm spirit and acrobatic saves. The positive attitude of Fleury is a unique quality for a position where confidence is continuously needed.

Facts

442. Fleury assisted the Pittsburgh Penguins in winning three championships.

443. He participated in the inaugural season of the Vegas Golden Knights and guided them to the Stanley Cup Finals.

444. In 2010, he won the gold medal at the Olympics with Team Canada.

445. He holds the NHL record for most victories in shootouts.

446. He is one of the most resilient goalies around, rarely missing a night off.

Mitch Marner–The Playmaking Dynamo

Equipped with a boyish charm, a soothing smile, and a beautiful aura, young Mitch Marner is truly a playmaking genius for the Toronto Maple Leafs. His unique style revolves around exceptional creativity and playmaking skills, not forgetting his amazing speed, which makes him a constant threat to the opponents on the ice.

Facts

447. In the 2015 NHL Draft, he was chosen fourth overall, which sparked discussions about his potential.

448. His father and uncle, both professional hockey players, started a family tradition.

449. He gives $1000 to charity at every point via his Marner Assist Fund.

450. He became the franchise's youngest-ever player to score 300 points in a career

451. He led the OHL's London Knights to a Memorial Cup victory.

Connor Bedard–The Junior Prodigy

The junior prodigy who's making waves in the WHL is Connor Bedard. As a teenager, he has marked a strong career in hockey by showcasing the utmost talent and scoring ability. He is known as the first player with a unique status in the WHL. This dude is worth the hype.

Facts

452. At 15, he was given exceptional player status, allowing him to be picked early in the WHL draft.

453. Bedard became the first player in WHL history to have scored 25 goals in a season at the age of 15.

454. He demonstrated his global prowess by competing for Canada in the Youth Olympics.

455. He broke multiple youth league scoring records, indicating a promising future.

456. He became a first-round pick in the WHL draft, confirming his elite prospect status.

Cale Makar–The Blueline Dynamo

The Colorado Avalanche is fiercely powerful when it has Cale Maker. His confidence and athleticism redefine his role as a defenseman in the NHL.

Facts

457. Makar was named the top college hockey player and received the Hobey Baker Award.

458. In the regular season and the playoffs, he set records for the most points scored by a rookie defenseman.

459. Makar made an instant impression after making the leap from college to the NHL.

460. He had a major impact on the Avalanche's Stanley Cup run.

461. He is a threat in every zone because of his remarkable skating ability.

Trevor Zegras–The Playful Visionary

With a twinkle in his eyes and a mischievous grin, Trevor Zegras is a legitimate, playful visionary for Anaheim Ducks. Just at the age of 21, Zegras has marked his style with a broad vision, creativity, and puck-handling skills.

462. He won MVP honors with Team USA at the 2021 World Junior Championships (Yuzyk & Seidner, 2022).

463. He prospered at Boston University, winning praise for his outstanding college production.

464. He made an instant impression when he joined the NHL with the Anaheim Ducks.

465. He grew up playing hockey in the competitive Michigan hockey scene.

466. Zegras is renowned for interacting with fans off the rink by posting amusing and lighthearted moments on social media.

Part V

Hockey Chronicles: Legends, Rivalries, and Frozen Feats

Dynasties: Hockey's Kingdoms of Greatness

Some hockey teams have ruled the realm for a long time. Teams today still get inspiration from their legendary feats. Let's find out about their tales.

467. From 1956-1960, the Montreal Canadiens set an NHL record-setting five straight Stanley Cup victories.

468. In five years in the 1980s, the Edmonton Oilers, under the captaincy of Wayne Gretzky, won four Stanley Cups.

469. Hockey dynasties frequently produce legendary players who have become household names.

470. During their dynasty in the early 1980s, the New York Islanders won a record 19 straight playoff series.

471. Hockey's history and culture are shaped by dynasties that leave a long-lasting legacy.

Rivalries: Clash of the Titans on Ice

What's a game without rivalries? The hockey heroes do have fierce battles with each other. Let's hear some epic facts about it.

472. One of the most intense team rivalries, spanning several decades, is that between the Boston Bruins and Montreal Canadiens.

473. The two teams have been rivals for the last 20 years, with Canada holding 20 gold medals in comparison to the five gold medals held by the United States.

474. Mario Lemieux and Wayne Gretzky had a cordial but fierce rivalry that drove each other to achieve greater things.

475. Famous incidents, such as the "Miracle on Manchester" involving the Kings and Oilers, were frequently the result of rivalries.

476. The Edmonton Oilers and Calgary Flames have a storied rivalry known as the Battle of Alberta.

Crazy Stats: Numbers That Boggle the Mind

Hockey statistics possess an almost mystical quality, acting as enchanting spells that expose the extraordinary achievements of players. These stats can be likened to wizardry, with players conjuring up mesmerizing acts on the ice. Whether it's scoring records or mind-boggling save percentages, these statistical insights truly transform hockey into a spellbinding spectacle.

477. The legendary Martin Brodeur holds the record for most shutouts in NHL history during his career.

478. With an astounding 215 points in a season, Wayne Gretzky holds the record for most points in a single season.

479. Bill Mosienko recorded the fastest hat trick in NHL history, with just 21 seconds.

480. Wayne Gretzky has the longest point streak in NHL history, with 51 games in a row.

481. In 1988, Mario Lemieux scored five goals in five different ways in a single NHL game.

Trophies: Hockey's Shiny Treasures

Trophies are the crowns that are placed on the heads of hockey kings. The bravest and most skilled warriors get this jewel. Every trophy has its own tale; let's hear about them.

482. Dating back to 1893, the Stanley Cup is the oldest trophy still given to professional athletes.

483. Lord Stanley of Preston, Canada's Governor General, first bought the Stanley Cup in 1892 as a challenge cup for the country's greatest amateur hockey team.

484. Each year, the Stanley Cup gets engraved with the names of the victorious team's players, coaches, management, and staff. It may accommodate up to 13 victorious teams until a new ring is required.

485. The Cup has been around for over 125 years, and its history is replete with stories of triumph, sadness, and even adventure. It was stolen twice, in 1905 and 1970, but was found both times.

486. The Stanley Cup Playoffs' most valuable player, who displays clutch play, is given the Conn Smythe Trophy.

487. The Vezina Trophy is given to the best goalie in the league; past winners include Dominik Hasek and Patrick Roy.

488. Recipients of the Calder Memorial Trophy, which recognizes the rookie of the year, frequently go on to become future superstars.

489. Past winners of the Hart Trophy, which goes to the most valuable player in the league, include Wayne Gretzky and Mario Lemieux.

Winter Classic: Hockey's Frozen Spectacle

Just as the Yule Ball was a grand fest in Hogwarts, the Winter Classic is also a great event held on a frozen lake. It's a hockey carnival where teams from all around the world gather and battle the game in front of thousands of cheering fans.

490. With the Buffalo Sabres and Pittsburgh Penguins, Ralph Wilson Stadium hosted the inaugural Winter Classic in 2008.

491. Outdoor hockey games honor the sport's early years, when players skated on frozen ponds.

492. Famous locations like Notre Dame Stadium and Fenway Park are frequently used for the Winter Classic.

493. This has turned into a yearly tradition on New Year's Day, drawing families together to take in the spectacle.

494. Winter Classic competitions are renowned for their distinct ambiance and unforgettable moments.

Iconic Arenas: The Majestic Palaces of Hockey

Hockey palaces have their own charm and stories for everyone who loves this game. Let's hear them out.

495. The New York Rangers' home arena, Madison Square Garden, is the oldest NHL venue still in operation.

496. The Bell Centre in Montreal is renowned for its fervent supporters, who foster an exceptional and electrifying atmosphere.

497. One well-known custom at the United Center in Chicago is for spectators to applaud while the national anthem is playing.

498. San Jose's "Shark Tank" (SAP Center) is well-known for its lively patrons and shark-themed events.

499. As the former home of the Maple Leafs, Toronto's "Barn on Dale" (Maple Leaf Gardens) has historical significance.

Amazing Records: Feats That Defy the Laws of Hockey

This part is the most fun and exciting, where new achievements are made and older ones become an inspiration. Let's hear about unbreakable goal scorings and unbeatable winning streaks.

500. Wayne Gretzky's career total of 2,857 points (goals plus assists) still holds a record today.

501. The Pittsburgh Penguins have the longest winning streak in NHL history at 17 consecutive victories during the 1992-1993 season.

502. Phil Kessel set an all-time NHL record of 1,064 straight games played in the regular season.

503. Teemu Selanne accomplished an incredible feat when he scored a rookie record of 76 goals in a single season.

504. The Boston Bruins (1928–1929) were an offensive powerhouse, averaging 3.5 goals per game at the time.

Conclusion

This book is no less than an enchanting journey that will take you the exciting stories of hockey, where you will read about legendary players, amazing comebacks, and interesting trivia. Remember, this sport is more than just a game—it's a profound experience that is full of passion, friendship, and memories that will stay with you forever.

No matter what your aspirations are in the world of hockey, be it scoring the ultimate winning goal, showing off your impeccable defense skills, or simply being a passionate supporter from the stands, one thing is for sure: the attraction and unity that hockey brings are undeniable.

Embrace the thrill of keeping the puck sliding, the blades effortlessly gliding, and the echoes of cheers ringing throughout. You're not just a spectator; you are an integral part of hockey's captivating story that knows no bounds! Apart from your education and other responsibilities, let the breeze touch your game, let the world witness what a tremendous player you are, and let the hockey stick be your magic broom!

"Your Opinion Matters to Us!"

We hope you are happy and satisfied with this book! Help us gauge how well we are connecting with our audience by leaving feedback. This will allow us to continually refine and enhance our offerings for our dear readers. As dedicated authors, we invest our total commitment to crafting every single page.

We sincerely hope that kids of this generation become more interested in books than their phones. Our goal in coming up with **500+ Fun & Fascinating Hockey Facts for Kids** is to create an engaging and educational reading material that not only triggers their curiosity but also sparks a deep appreciation for the game.

We genuinely value your thoughts, comments, and suggestions more than you can imagine. Feel free to let us know what you like the most about this book, what should not have been added, and what we could improve on for the next time. Your review not only shows support for our small initiative but also helps expand the thriving community of passionate hockey enthusiasts across the globe.

By sharing your insights and experiences, you add to the collective knowledge and enhance the overall experience for hockey fans. We are sincerely grateful for your support and the role you play in our journey.

Thank you in advance for taking the time to share your valuable feedback. We highly appreciate your contribution to the shaping of our future endeavors.

References

Adkisson D. (2022). *Cinderella Comebacks*. Mayorsmanor.com. https://mayorsmanor.com/2022/02/biggest-nhl-comebacks-of-all-time/

Bachynski, K. E. (2020). Too Rough for Bare Heads: The Adoption of Helmets and Masks in North American Ice Hockey, 1959–79. *Sport History Review, 51*(1), 25–45. https://doi.org/10.1123/shr.2019-0026

Bekkering, D. J. (2014). Of "Lucky Loonies" and "Golden Pucks" *Studies in Religion/Sciences Religieuses, 44*(1), 55–76. https://doi.org/10.1177/0008429814548172

Beneteau, J. (2023). *Remember When? Bobby Orr flies through air after winning Stanley Cup*. Www.sportsnet.ca. https://www.sportsnet.ca/hockey/nhl/remember-bobby-orr-flies-air-winning-stanley-cup/

Bertovich, Y. (2019). The Untold Stories of Female Athletes. In *Google Books*. Atlantic Publishing Company. https://books.google.com.pk/books?hl=en&lr=&id=pZSFDwAAQBAJ&oi=fnd&pg=PA1&dq=Manon+Rh%C3%A9aume+was+the+first+woman+to+play+as+a+goalie+in+NHL+game+in+1992.&ots=PSvVRlLmoD&sig=AWpw_LlxHsL6ZPnUfSwZ7GldRvo&redir_esc=y#v=onepage&q&f=false

Blumberg, Z., Markovits, A., & Schnoll, A. (2020). A History of America's Aversion to Tie Games in Popular Team Sports. *International Journal of the Sociology of Leisure, 3*(2), 153–175. https://doi.org/10.1007/s41978-020-00053-4

Botte, P., & Hahn, A. (2003). Fish Sticks: The Fall and Rise of the New York Islanders. In *Google Books*. Sports Publishing LLC. https://books.google.com.pk/books?hl=en&lr=&id=Yy803cx0zhYC&oi=fnd&pg=PA1&dq=The+Zamboni+of+the+New+York+Islanders+was+a+unique+float+in+their+1980+victory+parade.&ots=uy-kfs26cs&sig=dXYZKRtw6Vo3tu38g62RCmx1f4k&redir_esc=y#v=onepage&q&f=false

Brown, J. (2019). *Looking Back at the Original Bruins vs. Blues Stanley Cup Battle*. Boston University. https://www.bu.edu/articles/2019/tom-whalen-on-bobby-orr-stanley-cup/

Campbell, K. (2021). *To be honest, Marie-Philip Poulin is clutch*. Hockey Unfiltered with Ken Campbell. https://kencampbell.substack.com/p/to-be-honest-marie-philip-poulin

Coenen, C. R. (2016). J. Andrew Ross.Joining the Clubs: The Business of the National Hockey League to 1945. *The American Historical Review, 121*(3), 949–950. https://doi.org/10.1093/ahr/121.3.949

Cox, D., & Joyce, G. (2010). The Ovechkin Project: A Behind-the-Scenes Look at Hockey's Most Dangerous Player. In *Google Books*. John Wiley and Sons. https://books.google.com.pk/books?hl=en&lr=&id=Kz3ear72iyYC&oi=fnd&pg=PT6&dq=One+of+the+most+celebrated+goals+of+history+is+when+Alex+Ovechkin+scored+%22The+Goal%22+against+the+Phoenix+Coyotes+in+2006.+&ots=k8hTnaZH6M&sig=Z916Cfe1NrmVNbDeLA-mXLVYNSM&redir_esc=y#v=onepage&q&f=false

Dalum, M. (2016). 2017 NHL Winter Classic. *Master of Arts in Sport Management*. https://digitalcommons.csp.edu/sport-management_masters/22/

Davidson, N. (2023). *Bobby Baun, who scored OT goal on broken leg to win 1964 Stanley Cup, dead at 86*. CBC. https://www.cbc.ca/sports/hockey/nhl/bobby-baun-death-maple-leafs-stanley-cup-nhl-1.6936604

Denault, T. (2012). A Season in Time: Super Mario, Killer, St. Patrick, the Great One, and the Unforgettable 1992-93 NHL Season. In *Google Books*. John Wiley & Sons. https://books.google.com.pk/books?hl=en&lr=&id=OPygOqLbFuAC&oi=fnd&pg=PR1&d q=Darryl+Sittler+set+a+new+NHL+record+in+1976+for+maximum+points+in+one+gam e+by+scoring+six+goals+and+helping+on+four+others.+&ots=-dBgUtQ81h&sig=UY_KCeFeivC2xCywzoSimyzNn5I&redir_esc=y#v=onepage&q&f=false

Diamond, D., Duplacey, J., & Zweig, E. (2003). The Ultimate Prize: The Stanley Cup. In *Google Books*. Andrews McMeel Publishing. https://books.google.com.pk/books?hl=en&lr=&id=rEIqYOxqDDMC&oi=fnd&pg=PA3& dq=how+old+is+stanley+cup&ots=GJ_hbfSEcB&sig=UsnQOt7MMqb8j97ky776uAYgwY4 &redir_esc=y#v=onepage&q=how%20old%20is%20stanley%20cup&f=false

Eichel, M. (2011, June 6). *Stanley Cup Finals 2011: Top 5 Stanley Cup Final Comebacks*. Bleacher Report. https://bleacherreport.com/articles/725000-2011-stanley-cup-finals-top-5-stanley-cup-final-comebacks

Falcon, L. (2011, February 22). *1980 Miracle on Ice: Greatest Moment in Sports History Will Never Get Old*. Bleacher Report; Bleacher Report. https://bleacherreport.com/articles/568574-1980-miracle-on-ice-greatest-moment-in-sports-history-will-never-get-old

Gillis, S. (1996). Putting it on ice : a social history of hockey in the Maritimes, 1880-1914. *Library2.Smu.ca*. https://library2.smu.ca/handle/01/22519

Gzowski, P. (2004). The Game of Our Lives. In *Google Books*. Heritage House Publishing Co. https://books.google.com.pk/books?hl=en&lr=&id=LKR2iebOl4wC&oi=fnd&pg=PA8&dq =In+five+years+in+the+1980s

Harrison, R. (2023, July 9). *NHL's 10 Most Impressive Streaks*. The Hockey Writers. https://thehockeywriters.com/nhl-ten-most-impressive-streaks/#:~:text=Wayne%20Gretzky

Hirshon, N. (2018). We Want Fish Sticks: The Bizarre and Infamous Rebranding of the New York Islanders. In *Google Books*. U of Nebraska Press. https://books.google.com.pk/books?hl=en&lr=&id=9dN5DwAAQBAJ&oi=fnd&pg=PR9& dq=During+their+dynasty+in+the+early+1980s

History of Hockey | FIH. (n.d.). Www.fih.ch. http://www.fih.ch/hockey-basics/history/#:~:text=The%20roots%20of%20hockey%20are

J.T. (2023, October 17). *The 23 Best NHL Coaches of All Time Ranked*. Hockey Topics. https://hockeytopics.com/the-best-nhl-coaches-of-all-time-ranked/

Johnson, D. (2023, November 21). *Bobby Orr's Flying Goal*. The Hockey Writers. https://thehockeywriters.com/bobby-orr-flying-goal-iconic/#:~:text=During%20the%20Boston%20Bruins%201969

Kessiby, M. (2023, April 21). *The Extraordinary Evolution of Hockey Equipment*. Montreal Science Centre. https://www.montrealsciencecentre.com/blog/the-extraordinary-evolution-of-hockey-equipment

Kirk, R. (2013, February 13). *The Most Impressive Streaks in NHL History*. Bleacher Report. https://bleacherreport.com/articles/1527696-the-most-impressive-streaks-in-nhl-history

Kurtzberg, B. (2012a, June 8). *The 100 Toughest Players in NHL History*. Bleacher Report. https://bleacherreport.com/articles/1212030-the-100-toughest-players-in-nhl-history

Kurtzberg, B. (2012b, June 19). *The 60 Best Nicknames in NHL History*. Bleacher Report. https://bleacherreport.com/articles/1225482-the-60-best-nicknames-in-nhl-history

Laroche, S. (2014). Changing the Game: A History of NHL Expansion. In *Google Books*. ECW Press. https://books.google.com.pk/books?hl=en&lr=&id=N4OFAwAAQBAJ&oi=fnd&pg=PT10 &dq=In+1936

Lennox, D. (2008). Now You Know Hockey: The Book of Answers. In *Google Books*. Dundurn. https://books.google.com.pk/books?hl=en&lr=&id=UCZghkj2gW4C&oi=fnd&pg=PA7&dq =In+1988

Leonetti, M. (2011). The Magnificent Mario. In *Google Books*. Scholastic Canada.
https://books.google.com.pk/books?hl=en&lr=&id=OlugzwOxnWIC&oi=fnd&pg=PR2&dq
=In+1988+Mario+Lemieux+made+a+record+by+scoring+five+goals+in+five+different+st
yles+in+a+single+game.&ots=yA6OXeztXy&sig=qYFHV5xTCt2wUioS_gPlLQ-
av28&redir_esc=y#v=onepage&q&f=false

Lockhart, A. (2023, July 19). *What have been some of the most horrific injuries in Ice Hockey?*
Thehockeyden.co.uk. https://thehockeyden.co.uk/what-have-been-some-of-the-most-horrific-
injuries-in-ice-hockey

Macnow, G., & Gargano, A. L. (2003). The Great Philadelphia Fan Book. In *Google Books*. B B& A
Publishers.
https://books.google.com.pk/books?hl=en&lr=&id=9hpr2i0iHNEC&oi=fnd&pg=PA9&dq
=In+1974+the+fans+of+Buffalo+Sabres+threw+so+many+souvenir+pugs+onto+the+field
+that+the+game+had+to+be+postponed.+&ots=JZAKGjk1K5&sig=kISR4J0aDWoOBit6E
1sLxvrdNyE&redir_esc=y#v=onepage&q&f=false

Melendez , A. (2020, May 20). *Today in Flyers History: Remembering the infamous Fog Game*. Broad Street
Buzz. https://broadstreetbuzz.com/2020/05/20/flyers-history-infamous-fog-game/

Myers, H. S. J., Bill Dow, Jason La Canfora and Gene. (2022, June 26). *Fight Night at The Joe: "Darren
McCarty will never pay for a meal in this town again."* Detroit Free Press.
https://www.freep.com/story/sports/mlb/tigers/2022/06/26/detroit-red-wings-colorado-
avalanche-fight-night-1997/7739708001/

Njororai, W. W. S. (2014). South Africa FIFA World Cup 2010: African Players' Global Labour
Distribution and Legacy. *African Football, Identity Politics and Global Media Narratives*, 71–90.
https://doi.org/10.1057/9781137392237_5

Phen, J. (2011, May 7). *50 Greatest Goaltenders in NHL History*. Bleacher Report.
https://bleacherreport.com/articles/690878-nhl-rankings-top-50-greatest-goaltenders-in-nhl-
history

Poniatowski, K. (2011). "You're Not Allowed Body Checking in Women's Hockey": Preserving
Gendered and Nationalistic Hegemonies in the 2006 Olympic Ice Hockey Tournament. *Women
in Sport and Physical Activity Journal*, *20*(1), 39–52. https://doi.org/10.1123/wspaj.20.1.39

Price, N. G. (2020). Hockey is For Everyone holds the key to hockey's racism problem.
Repositories.lib.utexas.edu. https://repositories.lib.utexas.edu/items/4804478a-9a0e-4568-b2d6-
d7ea51fe0f53

Ranft, A. L., & Smith, A. D. (2020, January 10). *"You miss 100% of the shots you don't take."*
Www.elgaronline.com; Edward Elgar Publishing.
https://www.elgaronline.com/display/edcoll/9781789902815/9781789902815.00023.xml

Ryan, J., & Lieser. (2008). *The Real Cold War: The Athletic Arena of the Olympic Games - ProQuest*.
Www.proquest.com.
https://www.proquest.com/openview/64316685d868531ef1479fda3a4861c3/1?pq-
origsite=gscholar&cbl=18750&diss=y

Smith, P. B. (2022, December 18). *Marie-Philip Poulin makes history by winning Canada's Athlete of the Year
award*. Infobae. https://www.infobae.com/aroundtherings/articles/2022/12/18/marie-philip-
poulin-makes-history-by-winning-canadas-athlete-of-the-year-award/

Smith, S. (2019, June 11). *Document - Gale Academic OneFile*. Go.gale.com.
https://go.gale.com/ps/i.do?id=GALE%7CA588430881&sid=googleScholar&v=2.1&it=r&li
nkaccess=abs&issn=03624331&p=AONE&sw=w&userGroupName=anon%7E3fd3e383&at
y=open-web-entry

Staff, F. (2022, May 28). *Get Motivated With Some Great Hockey Quotes*. FloHockey.
https://www.flohockey.tv/articles/7971329-get-motivated-with-some-great-hockey-quotes

Szto, C., Pegoraro, A., Morris, E., Desrochers, M., Emard, K., Galas, K., Gamble, A., Knox, L., &
Richards, K. (2020). #ForTheGame: Social Change and the Struggle to Professionalize
Women's Ice Hockey. *Sociology of Sport Journal*, *38*(4), 1–10. https://doi.org/10.1123/ssj.2020-
0085

Unk, J. (2023, December 8). *The Top 10 Hockey Players of All Time*. HowTheyPlay. https://howtheyplay.com/team-sports/the-top-10-hockey-players-of-all-time

Yuzyk, M., & Seidner, P. (2022). E-Sports Competitions. *Studies in Systems, Decision and Control*, 671–716. https://doi.org/10.1007/978-3-030-97008-6_30

Zweig, E. (2006, February 7). *1972 Canada-Soviet Hockey Series (Summit Series)*. Www.thecanadianencyclopedia.ca. https://www.thecanadianencyclopedia.ca/en/article/1972-canada-soviet-hockey-series#:~:text=The%20series%20became%20as%20much

Images References

Barwich, B. (2017). *A group of people playing outdoor hockey during winter*. Unsplash. https://unsplash.com/photos/group-of-people-playing-outdoor-hockey-during-winter-yaAruHxQ9OQ

CA (2019). *Smiling boy photo*. Pexels. https://www.pexels.com/photo/smiling-boy-photo-2858934/

Dunncan1890 (2018). *Vintage engraving of Prince Albert Victor, duke of Clarence playing hockey at Cambridge*. iStock. https://www.istockphoto.com/vector/prince-albert-victor-duke-of-clarence-playing-hockey-gm943418140-257769977?phrase=duncan1890+hockey

Hewines, M. (2020). *Black white and red Nike shoes*. Unsplash. https://unsplash.com/photos/black-white-and-red-nike-shoes-s3BIuan-wjo

Maurice DT (2021). *A group of men playing a game of ice hockey*. Unsplash. https://unsplash.com/photos/a-group-of-men-playing-a-game-of-ice-hockey-Hecp8nMJU3A Korolkoff, A. (2017). *Ice hockey players on ice hockey arena*. Unsplash. https://unsplash.com/photos/ice-hockey-players-on-ice-hockey-arena-u5IPj3-f0XI

Musalimov, K. (2020). *People playing ice hockey on stadium*. Unsplash. https://unsplash.com/photos/grayscale-photo-of-people-playing-ice-hockey-U46JmHwcZp8

Parente, I. (2020). *Three persons playing ice hockey*. Unsplash. https://unsplash.com/photos/three-persons-playing-ice-hockey-sLMqgNQJx18

Petiard, M. (2020). *Ice Hockey Players on Ice Hockey Field*. Unsplash. https://unsplash.com/photos/ice-hockey-players-on-ice-hockey-field-W7t3cNm8LXk.

Walker, A. (2024). *A group of people playing a game of ice hockey*. Unsplash. https://unsplash.com/photos/a-group-of-people-playing-a-game-of-ice-hockey-EoX5NjDDnu8

Made in United States
Orlando, FL
12 December 2024

55527809R00055